TO NICK & TIM AND SUNAPEE MEMORIES
—LIZI BOYD

Library of Congress Cataloging-in-Publication Data:

Boyd, Lizi, 1953- author. Flashlight / by Lizi Boyd.
pages cm
Summary: In this story without words, a boy explores
the woods after dark with a flashlight.
ISBN 978-1-4521-1894-9 (alk. paper)
1. Boys—Juvenile fiction. 2. Flashlights—Juvenile fiction.
3. Night—Juvenile fiction. 4. Stories without words.
[1. Flashlights—Fiction. 2. Night—Fiction.
3. Stories without words.] I. Title.

PZ7.B6924Fl 2014
[E]—dc23

2013029635

Manufactured in China.

Design by Lizi Boyd and Sara Gillingham Studio.
Typeset in Oyster.
The illustrations in this book were rendered in gouache.

10 9 8 7 6 5 4 3 2 1

Chronicle Books LLC
680 Second Street
San Francisco, California 94107

Chronicle Books—we see things differently.
Become part of our community at www.chroniclekids.com.

# FLASHLIGHT

## LIZI BOYD

chronicle books · san francisco